A Possum's Pyramid &
THE TOMB OF
KING TUT

A Possum's Pyramid &
THE TOMB OF
KING TUT

written by
Jamey M. Long

TATE PUBLISHING *& Enterprises*

Published by Tate Publishing & Enterprises, LLC
127 E. Trade Center Terrace | Mustang, Oklahoma 73064 USA
1.888.361.9473 | www.tatepublishing.com

Tate Publishing is committed to excellence in the publishing industry. The company reflects the philosophy established by the founders, based on Psalm 68:11,
"The Lord gave the word and great was the company of those who published it."

Book design copyright © 2009 by Tate Publishing, LLC. All rights reserved.
Cover and Interior design by Kellie Southerland
Illustration by Brandon Wood

Published in the United States of America

ISBN: 978-1-60696-293-0
1. Juvenile Fiction, Historical, Ancient Civilizations
2. Animals, General
09.03.17

DEDICATION

This book is dedicated to my uncle Ken. May you always keep your sense of adventure and your love for life.

On the edge of a small northern town there was a forest. The year was 1922, and a possum was waking up to a beautiful summer moonlit night. Opie was hanging cozily from his favorite tree branch high above the ground by his long pink tail. As Opie woke up, he untangled his tail from the tree branch. He stretched out his furry little arms and let out a big yawn. Opie sat up on his tree branch and looked out over the big evergreen forest. He always liked this time of night when the forest was at its quietest. Opie would listen to the quiet forest and all of the sounds the trees and leaves made in the gentle wind.

"What a beautiful night," said Opie as he looked up at the moon. "I feel like going on an adventure. But where should I go?" Opie thought long and hard about where he should go for his adventure. As he was thinking, he thought about his friend the boy and began to smile and laugh. Opie had always enjoyed visiting the boy and had many fun adventures with him in the past. Opie had made up his mind. "I will go and visit the boy," Opie exclaimed.

Opie climbed down his tree and scurried through the forest. Opie traveled all night, only stopping to play with a few of his forest friends along the way. Opie had been walking for quite a long time. As Opie came to the edge of the forest, the sun was beginning to shine through the trees. At the edge of the forest, Opie could see the boy's home. Opie looked around to see if there was anyone around and began walking through the high green grass in the boy's backyard.

As Opie walked closer to the boy's back porch, he saw the boy walking inside his house with his mother and father. Opie was a very curious possum, and he wanted to know what was going on.

I wonder what is going on, thought Opie. *I need to move closer so I can find out.* Opie made his way up to the boy's back porch and scampered over to the back door. The door was cracked open just far enough for Opie to see inside.

Opie stood up on his hind legs and poked his furry head inside the boy's house. As Opie looked around, he saw the boy and his parents packing for what looked to be a long trip.

"Is everything packed?" the boy's father asked.

"Everything is almost packed and ready for our trip to Egypt," the boy replied. "There is only one suitcase left upstairs. I will finish packing it and will bring it down."

A long trip, Opie thought to himself. *I wonder where the boy and his family are going. Wherever Egypt is, I want to go too!*

The boy walked up the stairs to finish packing his suitcase.

I do not have much time, Opie thought. He quickly crawled up the stairs and ran into the room with the boy and the suitcase. Opie scurried under the bed and was quietly watching the

boy. As the boy turned to grab more clothes to pack, Opie ran out from under the boy's bed and climbed up the bedpost. He then crawled into the suitcase and hid under some of the boy's shirts. He managed to do all of this without being seen and before the boy finished his packing.

"This should be everything I need for the trip," the boy said as he closed the suitcase. The boy then carried the suitcase downstairs and out to the car, unaware that Opie was hiding inside.

Inside the suitcase Opie chuckled. *This is a great hiding place*, Opie thought. *I cannot wait to find out exactly where we are going. This is certainly going to be a fun adventure.* Just then, Opie heard the boy and his family get into the car. The car engine started, and Opie knew they were now on their way.

After a long morning drive, the boy and his family finally stopped. They had arrived at a large shipping dock. They got out of the car and took their suitcases out of the trunk. The boy and his family began walking up the dock to a large Mediterranean passenger liner. The boy's father handed the ship's steward their boarding passes. Then they made their way onto the ship.

The ship was very large. They boy and his family had to go down many corridors before they finally found their room. The boy opened the door and put his suitcase on the floor next to his bed. He then went with his parents to explore the rest of the ship.

As the boy and his family were leaving to explore the ship, Opie was still hiding in the suitcase. The boy had packed his suitcase so full that one side of the zipper had popped open, allowing Opie to be able to crawl out. Opie ran to the door and saw the boy and his family walking down the hall and up to the main deck of the ship. He quickly ran down the hallway to follow them, still being careful not to be seen.

The boy and his family were on the main deck and looked over the railing at the large body of water below. They were sailing on the English Channel. Opie moved closer to the edge of the ship and climbed up on the railing. As he looked over the edge, he saw bright blue water as far as his eyes could see. As he looked closer at the water, he saw dolphins and other big fish swimming alongside of the ship. The boy also saw the dolphins and was pointing at them too.

After being on the main deck for a while, the boy and his family were hungry.

"I am hungry," said the boy. "Is it time for dinner?"

"Yes," replied the boy's father. "Let's go have dinner."

Opie's ears perked up at the sound of food. He loved food and loved to eat.

I am hungry too, thought Opie. *Let's eat!* Opie took off following the boy and his family to eat dinner. After eating a large dinner, the boy and his family were full. Opie also had a large, round belly, as he snuck all the leftovers when no one was looking. When dinner was over, everyone headed back to their rooms on the ship and settled down for a good night's sleep.

After traveling on the passenger liner for several days, the boy and his family arrived in Italy. In Italy the boy and his family got on another passenger ship that was headed to Alexandria, Egypt. After many more days of traveling, the boy and his family finally arrived in Egypt. When the boy and his family—and Opie—stepped off the ship's gangway, they quickly noticed something different. The ground was not hard and cold as it was in London. Instead, the ground was golden brown and very soft. It reminded Opie of the dirt ground in his forest. Egypt's ground was made of sand. Opie liked the feel of the sand on his paws. He began playing and wildly swinging his tail, making patterns in the sand.

I like Egypt already, thought a very happy and playful Opie.

"What will we do now that we have arrived in Egypt?" the boy asked his father.

"That is a good question, son," replied the boy's father. "We came to Egypt to work for Howard Carter."

"Who is Howard Carter?" asked the boy. Opie was glad the boy had asked this question. Opie was a very smart little possum but did not know who this person was.

"Howard Carter is an archeologist from London," said the boy's father.

An archeologist, thought a confused Opie. *I wonder what that is.*

"What does an archeologist do?" asked the boy, who followed his family and Howard Carter into a tent full of artifacts.

"An archeologist is an explorer who looks for precious relics from an ancient civilization."

If Howard Carter is in Egypt, and the boy and his family traveled all the way here, thought Opie, *there must be some ancient treasure from an old civilization to find. This is going to be very exciting! I cannot wait to go exploring for ancient relics and treasure.*

"Are there any ancient civilizations in Egypt?" the boy asked.

"Yes, Egypt has some of the oldest civilizations and ancient treasures in the world," replied the boy's father.

"Are we going to help Howard Carter look for these civilizations and ancient relics?" the boy asked his father.

"Yes, we are," said the boy's father. "However, we still have a long journey ahead of us. Starting tomorrow, we must travel along the Nile River. It is the longest river in the world and the only river that flows north. The river will lead us to the ancient kingdoms of Egypt. Now it is time to get some sleep. Goodnight, son."

"Goodnight," replied the boy.

As excited as Opie was about looking for ancient civilizations, he was also very tired from the long journey.

"Goodnight," said Opie as he laid his head down on the soft, sandy ground, yawned, and quickly fell asleep.

Before Opie knew it, it was morning and the sun was shining brightly in the sky. The boy and his family had just finished eating breakfast when they were greeted by a strange man. The man was tall, thin, and had a big, bushy mustache. He was wearing a white shirt with a tie under a dark black suit. He was also wearing a tall black hat.

"Greetings," said the man to the boy's family.

Opie curiously looked at the man.

I wonder if this is Howard Carter, thought Opie.

"Welcome to Egypt," continued the man as he stretched out his arm to shake the hand of the boy's father. "My name is Howard Carter. I am

happy to work with you in the search of ancient Egyptian treasure. Once you are ready, we can be on our way."

"We are ready to go!" exclaimed the boy, who could barely hold back his excitement. The boy's father and Howard Carter both laughed and packed up their things. Opie was also excited and could not resist yelling, "I am ready to go too!" Luckily, no one heard him because they were too busy packing for their trip down the Nile River.

"What will we be traveling on?" the boy asked Howard Carter.

That is a good question, thought Opie. It would be a long walk down the Nile River.

Howard Carter raised his hand and pointed behind him at some strange-looking animals that were standing behind him. The animals were brown, had two humps, and long necks. Opie was pretty familiar with most animals that lived in the forest, but he had never seen any animals that looked like this before.

What kind of animals are those? Opie wondered.

"Are those camels?" asked the boy.

"Yes, they are," replied Howard Carter.

"I have always wanted to see a camel," said the boy excitedly as he ran over to pet one. "I have only seen pictures of them in books. I can not believe that I am actually going to get to ride on one."

The boy's father helped the boy by grabbing his belongings and placing them on the second hump of his camel. Once the boy climbed on his camel, Opie quickly scurried over and climbed up the camel's second hump. He was sitting high on the camel's hump behind the boy and was ready to join the boy on his adventure.

The boy and his family, Howard Carter, and Opie traveled all day. Opie was having the time of his life. He had never seen so many different and wonderful things. Along the Nile River they saw many different Egyptian villages. Most Egyptians were farmers. They lived in houses made of mud bricks. The people wore clothes that were made of linen and did not wear shoes. Many of the Egyptian people kept animals as pets, and their children happily played with them all day long.

The Egyptians were simple people. They worked as artists and craftspeople making pottery, clothing, ships, leather, and jewelry. As they continued to travel down along the river, the boy and Opie saw many other unusual animals. They saw birds, hippos, lions, bulls, jackals, and even crocodiles.

Animals were not the most amazing thing they saw on their journey down the Nile River. They soon came to the Valley of the Kings. The boy and his family, Howard Carter, and Opie came across some tall, extraordinary-looking buildings. The first building they came across was very large. It had a body of a lion and the head of a man.

That is a strange-looking building, thought Opie. *I wonder what it is.*

The boy was also curious about the building.

"What building is that?" the boy asked Howard Carter.

"That is known as the Great Sphinx," replied Howard Carter. "It was built to protect the pyramids of Giza." Some of the other buildings had four sides and came to a point at the top.

More strange buildings, thought Opie to himself. *I wonder what kind of buildings those are.*

"Do you know what those buildings are?" Howard Carter asked the boy.

"I think those are pyramids," replied the boy.

"That is right," said Howard Carter. "They are called step pyramids. Each stone weighs over four thousand pounds. The pyramids were stacked one stone at a time by workers using wooden rollers. They were built to look like rays of sunlight."

Opie was in awe at the magnificent sight. He had never seen anything like the pyramids before.

"Why were the pyramids built?" the boy asked Howard Carter.

"That is a good question," replied Howard Carter. "Pyramids were built as a burial chamber for the kings of Egypt. Once a king died, the people wrapped the king's body in strands of linen to protect it. Do you know what this practice is called?"

Opie did not know but was eager to find out.

"I am afraid I do not know," replied the boy. "What is it called?"

"It is called mummification," replied Howard Carter. "Once a king is wrapped in the strands of linen, it is called a mummy. The mummy is then placed in a sarcophagus, or a stone coffin, which rests in a tomb."

I bet the tomb is buried inside of the pyramid, thought Opie.

"The tomb is buried inside of the pyramid," said Howard Carter.

Opie was very proud that he had figured that out.

I hope we get to go inside and explore a pyramid.

"Are we going to get to explore a pyramid?" the boy enthusiastically asked Howard Carter.

"Yes," replied Howard Carter. "That is why you and your family are here. I am looking for the tomb of King Tutankhamun."

"King Tut-a-what?" said Opie to himself.

"He is better known as King Tut," continued Howard Carter. "He was a young boy king, and his treasure is over three thousand three hundred years old. I hope to find his tomb so we can better understand what it was like to live during that time."

That is a very long time ago, thought Opie. *I*

wonder what it would be like to live back then as a king. I hope we can find his tomb and treasure so we can find out.

"Now it is getting late," said Howard Carter. "You and your family should get some rest. Tomorrow morning we start digging and looking for the tomb of King Tut."

After returning to their tent, the boy's mother and father quickly fell asleep. The boy and Opie were too excited about looking for King Tut's tomb, and they had a hard time falling asleep. However, they both eventually became too tired to stay awake any longer. Their eyes slowly closed, and the boy and Opie were soon fast asleep.

It was now November 4, 1922. The boy and Opie opened their eyes, and it was another sunny day. The boy and his family got their tools to begin excavating, or digging, for King Tut's tomb. Opie did not need tools to excavate. He was a natural digger. He quickly began digging in the sand with his paws. As Opie was digging in the shadows alongside the boy and Howard Carter, they made an important discovery. They had found the top step of a thirteen-step staircase that led down into the tomb. Everyone was very excited about their discovery and began shouting for joy. Opie was so excited that he began yelling too. Howard Carter, the boy and his family, and Opie began clearing the staircase that led to the tomb.

The boy grabbed a lantern, and they all walked down the staircase. When they reached the bottom of the steps, they ran into a mysterious plaster wall. The wall had ancient Egyptian seals and markings on it. Opie and the boy looked at all of the markings. Neither one of them recognized the writing on the wall.

"What kind of language is this?" the boy asked Howard Carter. "There are no words, only pictures."

"These pictures are known as hieroglyphics. It is one of the earliest forms of writing. Hieroglyphics use over seven thousand pictures and symbols."

As excited as everyone was to explore the tomb, they would unfortunately have to wait until the wall was carefully removed. This would take several days.

On November 26, Howard Carter and his team had finally cleared the twenty-six-foot corridor that was behind the plaster wall. However, they encountered another sealed entrance.

During the afternoon of November 27, Howard Carter, the boy and his family, and Opie were able to enter the tomb for the first time. The first room that they came to was called the antechamber. Howard Carter explained that this is always the first room in a tomb. It was filled with some jewelry and statues made of gold.

Opie was very excited. He could not wait for the boy and Howard Carter, and he went scurrying into the second room of the tomb. Opie looked back and saw that his footprints were being left in the sand. He did not want them to be seen so the boy and his family could make the discovery.

I wonder how I can hide my footprints, thought Opie. *I know what I can do!* As Opie continued to walk, he swung his tail back and forth to erase his trail.

The second room of the tomb was called the annex. The annex was full of lots of other fine Egyptian treasures. Opie looked around and saw beautiful pieces of jewelry and furniture. As he looked around the room, he did not see the tomb of King Tut; however, he did see another room that was hidden behind a secret chamber. It was the burial chamber.

Once again, Opie let his excitement get the best of him, and he ran into the next room.

"I wonder what this room is," said Opie as he eagerly looked around.

The walls of the room were covered with beautiful large paintings and shrines. As Opie walked through the room, he saw something sitting in the center of the room. He decided to walk over to see what it was. As Opie climbed on top of the strange object, he realized that this must be the sarcophagus for King Tut. Opie pushed with all his might until he slid the cover off the sarcophagus. Opie looked inside. Inside the sarcophagus was the mummy of King Tut.

"We have found the tomb of King Tut!" exclaimed Opie.

Opie was so excited that he went running back to get the boy and Howard Carter. As he approached the antechamber where he left them, he heard some voices that were not the boy's or

Howard Carter's. Opie snuck into the room and hid behind one of the statues. From behind the statue, Opie could see that there were some very bad men who were holding the boy, his family, and Howard Carter captive. They were tomb robbers who were going to steal all of King Tut's treasure.

Opie was a brave possum, and he knew that he had to save his friends.

"I must save my friends," said a determined Opie to himself. He quickly looked around the tomb and then had an idea. "I bet I can scare them away," exclaimed Opie. "And I know just how to do it."

Opie ran back into the burial chamber. He climbed inside of King Tut's sarcophagus and wrapped himself in some of the extra strands of linen that were lying next to King Tut. Opie wrapped himself in so many strands of linen that all that could be seen of him were his eyes, his ears, and his long pink tail sticking out behind him.

Opie walked back into the antechamber wrapped up in the linen strands. He began making loud moaning noises.

"What was that?" asked one of the tomb robbers.

"I don't know," replied one of the other tomb robbers. Just then, they saw a strange figure coming into the room. It was Opie wrapped up as a mummy.

"It's a mummy!" exclaimed the tomb robbers. "Let's get out of here!"

Opie chased the tomb robbers out of the tomb and made sure that they were long gone. When he returned to the tomb, everyone had made their way into the treasury room that led out of the burial chamber. Opie, the boy and his family, and Howard Carter had made one of the most significant discoveries of all time. They had found the tomb of King Tut. The treasure was truly priceless.

Howard Carter, the boy and his family, and Opie spent the next few years excavating the tomb. They illustrated, categorized, and restored the ancient artifacts. Once all of the artifacts were out of the tomb, they shared their discovery with the entire world. The artifacts were sent to the museum in Cairo for people all over the world to come and see.

Once all of the artifacts in the tomb of King Tut were excavated, it was time for the boy and his family to head back home. Opie was sad to leave Egypt, but he missed his friends and his home in the forest. The boy and his family said good-bye to their friend Howard Carter.

Howard Carter thanked them all for their help in finding the tomb of King Tut and gave them each a piece of treasure to keep. There was even a piece of Egyptian treasure for Opie.

After a long ship ride to Italy and across the English Channel, they finally arrived back home. Opie made sure that the boy and his family made it safely inside their home. He poked his head inside for one last look around.

"Good-bye," said Opie quietly to the boy and his family as he turned to leave. Opie crawled off the boy's porch and began walking through the backyard toward the forest. Opie thought about the adventure he had with the boy and was thankful for the wonderful time he had with his friends. He could not wait to tell his woodland friends all about it, and he scurried through the woods to his home in the forest.